The Intrepid Canadian
Expedition

FLAT STANLEY'S
WORLDWIDE ADVENTURES BOOK No. 4

The Intrepid Canadian
Expedition

CREATED BY **Jeff Brown**
WRITTEN BY Sara Pennypacker
PICTURES BY Macky Pamintuan

HARPER
An Imprint of HarperCollinsPublishers

Special thanks to
DANA BONSTROM

Flat Stanley's Worldwide Adventures: The Intrepid Canadian Expedition
Text copyright © 2010 by the Trust u/w/o Richard C. Brown a/k/a Jeff Brown f/b/o Duncan Brown.
Illustrations by Macky Pamintuan, copyright © 2010 by HarperCollins Publishers.
For information address HarperCollins Children's Books, a division of HarperCollins Publishers, 10 East 53rd Street, New York, NY 10022.
www.harpercollinschildrens.com

Library of Congress Cataloging-in-Publication Data
Pennypacker, Sara, 1951–
    The intrepid Canadian expedition / created by Jeff Brown ; written by Sara Pennypacker ; pictures by Macky Pamintuan. — 1st ed.
    p.   cm. (Flat Stanley's worldwide adventures ; 4)
    Summary: While acting as a snowboard, Stanley Lambchop gets carried away by a strong wind, sending him and his new friend Nick on a cross-country Canadian adventure.
    ISBN 978-0-06-142997-2 (trade bdg.) — ISBN 978-0-06-142996-5 (pbk.)
    [1. Adventure and adventurers—Fiction. 2. Snowboarding—fiction. 3. Canada—Fiction.] I. Brown, Jeff, 1926–2003. II. Pamintuan, Macky, ill. III. Title.
PZ7.P3856Int 2010   2009018295
[E]—dc22   CIP
                                                  AC

Typography by Alison Klapthor
10 11 12 13 14   LP/RRDC   10 9 8 7 6 5 4 3 2 1
❖
First Edition

CONTENTS

FLAT STANLEY's
WORLDWIDE ADVENTURES BOOK NO. 4

The Intrepid Canadian
Expedition

Stanley Goes Skiing

"Ha, ha!" Arthur Lambchop crowed as he skied past his older brother, Stanley. "Last one to the bottom is a frozen pancake!"

Stanley grunted as he dug his poles into the snow and strained against the frosty Canadian wind. Ever since he had awakened to find himself flattened by a bulletin board, Stanley had been putting up with Arthur's teasing about his shape. He didn't really mind—Arthur was a good brother: cheerful and loyal and a lot of fun.

And so what if being flat made it nearly impossible to ski? It had some mighty big advantages! For instance, Stanley could now travel by mailing himself anywhere in the world for a fraction of the cost of airfare. And he'd sure had a lot of adventures that would not have been available to a rounder boy!

His shape had been a big help to others, also. Stanley allowed himself a little smile of pride as he flapped another few feet down the slope. Wasn't his mother wearing her favorite ring because he had been able to slip down into a storm drain to retrieve it? Wasn't Abraham Lincoln's nose still in place at Mount Rushmore because he had turned himself into a human Band-Aid? And right now, weren't there a couple of museum sneak thieves playing poker in the city jail who were very sorry indeed they'd ever run into a boy flat enough to pose as a painting?

Just then Arthur whizzed by for a second time. "See you a-*ROUND!*" he shouted.

Stanley struggled harder against the wind and reminded himself even more firmly he should not feel sorry for himself. Why, already on this vacation his flatness had been an advantage: Because he could simply bend his legs at the knees, he had not needed to rent skis. With the money this had saved, the Lambchop family had enjoyed a hot chocolate party in the lodge the night before.

Stanley paused to catch his breath. Really . . . so what if he wasn't aerodynamic anymore? The sun was shining on the snowcapped mountains, and the air felt fresh on his cheeks. The scene spread below him was straight out of a winter wonderland postcard! Over on the expert trail, daredevils were enjoying the jumps, leaping and twisting in the air. In front of him, brightly dressed skiers swooshed by tall, frosted pines.

By the color of their parkas, Stanley recognized a band of kids he and Arthur had met the day before. He watched as his brother dashed down the mountain to them now. Everyone waved merrily to one another, and their shouts of greeting drifted up the mountain.

And there, in the middle of the trail, Stanley sank to the snow in defeat. He couldn't deny it anymore: Lately, his flatness had made him feel he just didn't have much in common with other people. Lately, it had made him feel lonely.

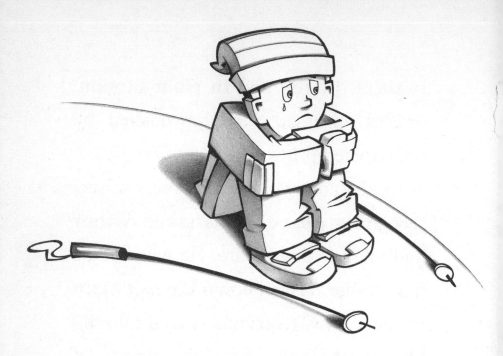

Tears froze on his eyelashes. Stanley brushed them off to watch Arthur and the other kids weave in and out of each other's paths, gliding gleefully down the mountain. Suddenly, though, Arthur shouted something and broke off from the group. He was heading toward the daredevil skiers!

Stanley scrambled to his feet. "No, Arthur!" he cried. "There are jumps!"

Too late! Stanley watched in horror as his brother flew up in the air and then crashed in a pinwheel of skis and poles and flying gloves!

Without a second thought, Stanley angled his body edgewise into the wind, like the blade of a knife. He ripped down the mountain at a terrifying speed, and within seconds he was at his brother's side.

"Are you all right?" Stanley asked. He offered Arthur his hand to help him up.

Just then a boy about Stanley's age skidded to a stop in a spray of snow beside the brothers. "Don't try to move him!" he warned. "He may have a broken bone. I'll go to get my father. . . . He's a doctor; he's on ski patrol today!" And then, just as suddenly, the boy took off on his snowboard again.

Stanley bent down beside his brother. "Does it hurt awfully?" he asked. "Do you want me to go get Mom and Dad?"

Arthur shook his head. "Just stay here with me until that fellow's father comes, all right?"

"Of course," Stanley promised. "I won't leave you."

Arthur's Accident

"Ah! Just breathe this fresh Canadian air, Harriet!" marveled George Lambchop to his wife. "I feel like a new man!"

Before Mrs. Lambchop could reply, a boy on a snowboard slooshed to a stop in a cloud of sparkling snow in front of them. "Are you Arthur and Stanley Lambchop's parents?" the boy asked.

"Oh, dear," Mrs. Lambchop fretted. "Is everything all right with the boys?"

"Arthur's had an accident. Follow me."

Mr. and Mrs. Lambchop hurried to follow the boy. In the lodge, they were alarmed to see Arthur on a couch, looking quite pale. His ankle was the size of a cantaloupe. A man in a white coat was bending over him, while Stanley looked on anxiously.

"Good gracious!" Mrs. Lambchop cried, flying to her son's side. "Are you all right, dear?"

Arthur winced. "It hurts a lot," he admitted. "But the doctor says it's just a bad sprain."

At this, the man in the white coat straightened and shook hands with the Lambchops. "The boy's lucky," he said. "He'll have to stay inside and heal for a few days, but then he'll be good as new."

"Stay *inside*?" Arthur cried. "No fair! Stanley and I have tickets for the World Snowboarding Championships this afternoon!"

"Out of the question, I'm afraid, young man."

Arthur slumped down with a groan, and the doctor turned back to Mr. and Mrs. Lambchop. "I'm Doctor Dave, by the way. It was my boy, Nick, who fetched you."

"Thank you so much for tending to our son," Mr. Lambchop said. "Perhaps we should give a call to Doctor Dan, the boys' regular doctor back home, to let him know what's going on. . . ."

"Doctor Dan? Not Doctor Dan of

America by any chance?"

When the Lambchops nodded, Doctor Dave smacked his forehead. "Well, it's a small world indeed!" he exclaimed. "Doctor Dan and I were roommates in medical school. What a cutup! And he's still got quite a sense of humor. Why, not long ago he wrote to say he was treating a most unusual case—Sudden Flatness Syndrome. As if anyone would believe he'd run into that!" Doctor Dave chuckled as he packed his bag. Mr. and Mrs. Lambchop looked at each other in confusion. "Our son Stanley is—" began Mr. Lambchop.

Doctor Dave ignored him and turned to Arthur. "Remember—complete bed rest, and get lots of exercise. Stay inside and breathe plenty of fresh air. Keep the leg up, and soak it in ice water—as hot as you can stand it."

"Hot ice water? Exercise and bed rest? I'm confused!" began Mrs. Lambchop.

"Perfectly natural," Doctor Dave said kindly. "Don't worry about it. After all, you're not a doctor." And then he left.

Stanley couldn't stand to see Arthur looking so glum. "I'll stay with you," he said. "We can play checkers."

Arthur heaved a big sigh. "No, you go. One of us might as well be there." He took a ticket out of his ski pants and held it out. "And take that boy Nick in my place. To thank him for helping me."

Stanley was moved by his younger brother's good sportsmanship. And, as he left to find Nick, he thought maybe this was just the opportunity he needed: Flat or not, he would make a new friend today!

3

Up, Up, and Away!

When Stanley and Nick arrived at the course, they noticed that most of the crowd was huddled near the bottom of the run. "The wind's picked up," said Nick. "It'll make for some fantastic boarding. But I wish we could get to the top to watch."

"Stay behind me and we'll fly right up," Stanley told Nick. With the wind at his back, Stanley towed his new friend to the start line.

"Thanks!" said Nick. "We'll have the best view in the place!"

The competition began and Nick was right—the conditions were perfect for some astonishing snowboarding.

"Did you see that fellow? That was an epic jump!" Nick said.

"You sure know a lot about this," Stanley said admiringly. "You must be really good."

"I'm better than good!" Nick bragged. He looked longingly down the trail. "In fact, if only I had my snowboard, I'd show them a thing or two. . . ."

Stanley grinned. "Well, there are some things I'm really good at, too. . . ." Then he stiffened, perfectly straight, with his arms at his side. "What do you think?"

Nick got the idea at once, but he smirked. "Are you serious? I only use the best boards! Very expensive . . . like the pros!"

"Oh, come on, let's try it," Stanley urged.

Nick rolled his eyes. "All right. Let's go!"

The boys edged their

way to a spot alongside the starting gate. Nick pulled on his goggles. "Ready?"

Stanley lay down in the snow and wrapped his scarf around his middle for foot bindings. "Ready!"

Nick jumped on top of him, and the starting gun went off. The boys shot down the slope, parallel to the other snowboarders. Nick called out commands, and Stanley positioned himself accordingly.

They made quite a team.

They started on course, weaving through packs of snowboarders as they fired over some moguls. "Are we in control?" Nick asked.

"I think so," Stanley replied as they

approached a ten-foot kicker jump.

"I hope so!" Nick hollered as they accelerated through the kicker, getting enormous air. The view from thirty feet above the slope was spectacular, peaceful, and still. Stanley caught a snowflake on his tongue, and then Nick said, "Stanley, we're going down now!" It was time for the landing, something that neither Nick nor Stanley had considered until that moment. They braced themselves for a rough impact, pleased when they glided gently into some thick powder, skidding away in a wake of snow. "That wasn't so bad," Stanley reflected.

"Stanley! Stanley!" Nick was pointing

ahead, trying his best to keep Stanley on course as they veered off the trail and into the woods!

"Look, a jib!" Nick said. He guided them toward a fallen tree where snowboarders were sliding over the trunk. They glided up and over the length of the log, spinning as onlookers admired their flair. "Wheeeeeee!" Stanley and Nick shouted together. They landed and sped back to the course, going faster than ever.

"Ladies and gentlemen, it seems we have a new challenger!" shouted the sports announcer. "And he's giving the professionals some competition!"

The wind blew even stronger now.

"I'm going to cut you into it now," Nick told Stanley. "If we can catch a current, I bet we can kill it!"

"Are you sure?" called out Stanley. "We're going higher than anyone else already!"

"That's just where I *should* be!" yelled Nick. "Bombs away!"

Stanley strained upward to catch the wind, remembering what he'd learned when Arthur had flown him like a kite. Up and up he went, while Nick crouched to hold on to Stanley with one hand. The crowd below roared in delight. Even the other snowboarders, finished with the run now, cheered in awe.

Stanley realized the problem first. "I can't come down!" he yelled to Nick. "I've caught the current, and I can't get out of it!"

Nick shouted, "No way, dude! I've got it under control." He tried to guide the Stanley-board down, but it was no use. . . . Suddenly, an even stronger gust of wind flipped them completely over. "Grab my hands and feet!" Stanley called to Nick.

Nick did, just in time, and Stanley allowed himself to billow in the wind like a parasail. The boys floated even higher over the course.

Far down below in the crowd, Stanley caught sight of his father, standing with

Doctor Dave, looking very worried.

"We're going to fall!" Nick screamed.

Both fathers gestured wildly with puzzled looks.

"No, we're not," Stanley tried to assure Nick. "Just don't let go!"

But Nick was panicking. "We're going

to fall!" he screamed even louder down to the dads. *"We're going to fall!"*

"No, not unless the wind were to stop all of a sudden," Stanley told Nick. "I'm not shaped for skiing anymore, but I'm just right for riding the air currents. Just hold on tight until the wind dies down, all right?"

Nick remained nervous, but he held tight. Up so high, it was curiously quiet, in spite of the wind.

Stanley decided to take Nick's mind off the situation by chatting. "My family is going to a wedding next week. It's somewhere near the Canadian border, so we decided to get a ski vacation in before it."

"That's nothing," Nick said. "I'm the ring bearer for a wedding next week!"

"We had a hot chocolate party at the lodge last night," Stanley tried.

"I drank four mugs yesterday," said Nick. "With extra marshmallows!"

"Then we watched a good show— about the Royal Canadian Mounted Police."

"I've seen every episode," Nick bragged.

No matter what Stanley mentioned, Nick had done it better, faster, or more times.

Stanley began to feel a little discouraged, but he kept talking all afternoon because it was working— Nick was relaxing.

As the sky darkened, the two boys grew tired. "You sleep a little first," Stanley offered. "One of us should always stay awake in case we come down."

Stanley steered them over the darkening mountains for a few hours as Nick dozed, then when the moon rose, Nick awoke and let Stanley close his eyes.

Stanley would have preferred to have his pillow and warm blankets at the lodge, with his brother in the next bed. But within minutes, he was sound asleep.

4

The Northwest
Territories

Stanley awoke to a poke in the ribs. The sun was shining brightly, and the wind had nearly stopped.

"We're coming down!" Nick shouted. "Fast!"

Stanley looked down. . . . Nick was right! They were hurtling toward a frozen landscape at a dangerous speed.

"Three, two, one . . . Roll!" Stanley cried. He arched his back even more—like a parachute—and they crashed softly to the ground, tumbling head over heels through snow and brush.

When they gathered themselves enough to sit up, they were stunned to find a man in a coat with a huge fur collar towering over them.

"An *Eskimo*!" Nick breathed.

"That's *Inuit*," the man corrected him, smiling.

"We're native people. I am Tulugaq."
He extended one hand to each boy and
pulled them to their feet easily. Beside
them, a furry dog was yapping and
dancing around.

"This is Amarok. It means 'wolf,' but he's very friendly. He watched you fall from the sky. . . . He's never seen birds as big as you!"

Nick straightened up. "I'm bigger than he is!"

Tulugaq frowned a little. "Well, no matter, you both look half frozen—follow me."

Nick and Stanley followed the Inuit man across the frozen tundra and into a little wooden house.

"Hey—you don't live in an igloo?" Nick asked.

Tulugaq rolled his eyes and laughed a hearty laugh. "There is a lot you don't know about my culture," the man said.

"Come inside and you will see that we are very modern."

Inside the house, Stanley and Nick were grateful to warm themselves by a roaring fire. Tulugaq introduced the boys to his wife, his grandmother, and half a dozen children who were scampering about, passing around bowls of caribou stew. The boys ate as Tulugaq told stories about his people.

Then, everyone was eager to hear the story of how Nick and Stanley had arrived.

"You traveled so far!" Tulugaq's grandmother marveled. "You floated right over the Rocky Mountains and into the Northwest Territories!"

"I steered," boasted Nick.

Tulugaq's wife patted Stanley's hand. "Your family must be very worried. Here, use our phone to call them, to let them know you are safe."

Stanley called the ski resort, eager to hear his parents' voices and to tell Arthur all about his adventure. "I'm sorry," the receptionist said. "The Lambchop family checked out yesterday."

Nick grabbed the phone. "How about my family? Connect me to Doctor Dave's room—it's the VIP suite!"

"Sorry," said the receptionist. "Doctor Dave and his party checked out yesterday also."

Stanley and Nick were too stunned to speak.

Tulugaq turned to his wife and said something in Inuit. Then he put his hand on Stanley's shoulder. "We must visit the shaman now. Come."

Stanley and Nick left with Tulugaq, still quite upset. Why would their families have left without them? And where could they have gone?

"The shaman is wise," Tulugaq told them as they traveled across the village. "He will have an answer."

But Nick and Stanley were not reassured. In fact, they were so worried, they barely even noticed that they traveled over a frozen river on a bridge of ice. *Where were their families?*

At last they came to a small, ancient hut. Tulugaq ducked inside and waved for the boys to follow him. In the dim light from an oil lamp, the boys could see that the walls were hung with animal furs and weavings and ancient artifacts.

Suddenly, one of the furs—huge, and with a monstrous mask on top—leaped to life and came straight for them!

The monster pulled off his mask to reveal . . . a very tiny, very wrinkled old Inuit man. He hugged Tulugaq and the two spoke for a moment in their language. Then Tulugaq pointed to the

boys and the old shaman turned. His eyes widened when he saw Stanley's shape. He walked all around him, eyeing him closely from all angles. The shaman seemed so impressed and respectful that Stanley didn't feel a bit embarrassed by all the curiosity.

Next the shaman handed a skin drum to Tulugaq. Tulugaq began to beat it, and the shaman began to chant and dance around the room. Faster and faster he whirled, almost as if he was in a trance.

Finally he spun to a stop and seemed to come back to himself. He smiled broadly, without a tooth in his head, and said something to Tulugaq.

"He says you boys are going to make a great journey together," Tulugaq translated. "You will go to the great falling waters. There, something will happen that will bond you to each other for life. Like brothers!"

"The great falling waters?" asked Nick. "Where's that?"

The shaman reached into a pouch he wore around his neck and pulled out a worn and creased postcard. He showed it to the boys.

"Niagara Falls!" Stanley cried. "I've heard of that! But how far away is it?"

"Near Toronto, in Ontario. Many

miles away," answered Tulugaq. "Thousands. Canada is a very large country."

Stanley and Nick exchanged looks—two boys on foot with no money could never travel that far.

Later that night, after a satisfying meal of dried fish and boiled walrus, the boys sat on the steps outside Tulugaq's home.

"Normally, I would just mail myself home," Stanley said. "But I don't think I should leave you here."

Nick nodded. "Besides," he said, "we don't know that there'd be anyone at our homes when we got there."

"I don't know what to do," Stanley said. "The shaman said we were supposed to make the journey together. Tulugaq says there's a dogsled to Calgary, where his cousin lives, but that's just a short part of the trip. . . ."

Both boys fell silent then, looking down at the frozen ground, discouraged.

After a while, though, Stanley—not being the kind of boy to give in to discouragement—looked up.

And then he gasped in disbelief! The night sky was shimmering with iridescent lights—neon greens and pinks and yellows danced across the entire horizon!

"The northern lights, Nick!" Stanley said at last. "It's a sign. If the whole sky can light up like that, I guess you and I can make our way to Niagara Falls somehow!"

Nick and Stanley shook hands. "We'll do it," they declared. "Like brothers!"

5

Mountie Martin

The next morning Stanley and Nick
said good-bye to their hosts and
found the dogsled team in the village.
There was only one seat, so Stanley
gamely volunteered to ride flat, under
everyone's feet. The ride was bumpy,
but every time he was tempted to
complain, Stanley recalled the magical
sky he and Nick had seen.

At last they arrived at the city of Calgary. The dogsled driver dropped them off at the address Tulugaq had provided. Stanley and Nick knocked.

When the door opened, Nick cried out, "This must be the wrong address! We're looking for Tulugaq's cousin."

"Cousin Tulugaq sent you? Well, come on in, little pardners! This is the spot, all right!"

"But how come you're not . . . How come you look like a cowboy?" Nick demanded—a little rudely, it must be said.

"And native people can't be cowboys, is that it? Well, guess again, little pardner. This is Calgary, the Wild West of Canada. I'm Nauja and I'm Inuit . . . and I'm also a cowboy! Now come on in from the cold and meet my family!"

"I guess I shouldn't have been surprised that a cousin of Tulugaq would be a cowboy," Stanley said thoughtfully after being introduced to Nauja's wife and children. "A girl I met at Mount Rushmore—Calamity Jasper—taught me that anyone can be a cowboy. She was part Lakota Sioux."

A smile came to Stanley's face remembering her. "She taught me some other things, too," he said. "Do you have a rope I could borrow?" Nauja brought a length of rope, and then Stanley entertained everyone with lariat tricks the cowgirl had shown him.

Nick sat in a corner, scowling. "Nobody likes a show-off, you know!" he muttered.

Just then a knock came at the door. There on the steps stood a man wearing a bright red coat, a big tan hat, and tall brown boots. He towered over everyone, so straight and powerful-looking, Stanley wondered for a minute if he was real.

Nauja gave the man a big bear hug. "Mountie Martin! What are you doing here, so far from Quebec?"

"Working. My partner and I chased

a dangerous desperado out here. I figure . . . I'm so close to *mon cher* cousin I might as well stop by for a quick visit . . . *non*?"

"You're Nauja's cousin, too? And Tulugaq's?" asked Nick.

"*Oui*. The French-Canadian side of the family, by marriage. Mountie

Martin, at your service," he saluted to the boys. "And who might you be?"

The boys introduced themselves and explained they were trying to get to Niagara Falls. Then Stanley asked what he was dying to know. "That dangerous desperado you were chasing . . . did you get him?"

The Mountie beamed. "But of course I got him, *mon ami*!" he cried. "I am a Royal Canadian Mounted Police officer. We always get our man! Now, how would you fellows like a ride to Quebec? My partner had to fly back with the desperado, and I could use the company. I could get you a lot closer to Niagara Falls."

Nick and Stanley made their good-byes and got into Mountie Martin's cruiser. The Mountie made adjustments to Stanley's seat belt until it held him snugly. "Safety first, eh? No matter the shape!"

Mountie Martin insisted they begin the trip with a big meal of Canadian specialties. "My treat," he said. "The United States of America is our neighbor. I am just being neighborly while you are visiting us!"

The boys—having the healthy appetites that travel brings on—enjoyed everything. Stanley's favorite was *poutine*. "French fries with cheese and gravy . . . what could be better?" he asked.

"Maple taffy," answered Nick. He poured more hot syrup over snow for a second helping of the sticky dessert.

Back on the road, Mountie Martin was a good guide. He pointed out mountains, rivers, and cities as they covered the vast and beautiful lands of Canada. All the sights seemed to remind him of a story or an interesting bit of history. Whatever he said, Nick seemed to already know about it.

On the second day, the conversation turned to sports. "Canada was a good choice for the 2010 Olympic Games," Mountie Martin said. "We are a nation of winter-sports lovers!"

At that, Nick listed all his favorites: skiing, skating, luging, and snowboarding. Nick was an expert at everything. Stanley slid down in his seat and stared out the window. At least, he thought, at least with every minute we are getting closer to Niagara Falls. And closer to home . . .

"How about you, Stanley?" Mountie Martin interrupted his thoughts. "Who's your favorite team?"

"Excuse me?"

"We were talking about hockey. Here in Canada, it is our national sport— the greatest sport in the history of the world!"

Stanley slid even farther down in his seat. "I've never seen a game," he mumbled, almost to himself.

"I'm a huge fan!" Nick exclaimed. "I've been to lots of games!"

Mountie Martin braked abruptly— but with caution and complete control. He pulled the cruiser over to the shoulder of the road and snapped the flashing lights on. "Safety first," he explained. "Now, would you please say that again, young man?"

Nick beamed. "I said I've been to lots of hockey games—I'm the biggest fan!"

"No, not you," the Mountie said. He nodded to Stanley. "You, *mon ami.* What did you just say?"

Stanley felt himself blush with embarrassment. "I've never been to a hockey game," he admitted.

"Well," said the Mountie, "here in

Canada, that is a very serious offense—a crime! And since I am a sworn officer of the law, I cannot let this crime continue. I'm afraid I'm going to have to arrest you and take you to a . . ."

Stanley gulped, waiting for his punishment.

". . . a hockey game!" Although Mountie Martin said this in a stern voice, he wore a big smile.

In the backseat, Stanley grinned and saluted. "Yes, sir, Mountie Martin, sir! I'm sorry for breaking the law!"

"No fair!" cried Nick. "I'm a bigger fan than he is!"

Mountie Martin turned to face Nick.

"A team that competes with itself is not a very strong team. You understand? *Oui?*"

"We?" Nick asked. "You mean Stanley and me, do we understand?"

"No," Mountie Martin began. "*Oui* means 'yes,' in French. But *oui*, I do mean you and Stanley. Look: You tell me stories about snowboarding as a pair, traveling across Canada together, flying through the air, relying upon each other. You make your way back across this whole country—again, because you are a team. Why must you always compete? In the Royal Canadian Mounted Police, we learn to rely on our partners. We must always be *we*. Now if you are ready to be a real team, I think I will take you *both* to this hockey game tonight!"

"Sure. For a hockey game, we'll be a team!" Nick smiled, but Stanley noticed he had crossed his fingers.

6

The Stanley Cup!

That night, as promised, Mountie Martin stopped in Ottawa and took the boys to a hockey game. "The Maple Leafs are playing. They're my favorite team, even though I am from Quebec," he admitted.

The game was as thrilling as Stanley had always heard. At halftime, a contest was announced. The fan with the best

sign would be invited down to the ice and given one chance to score a goal. If the fan made the shot—a one in a hundred chance—he or she would win a trip to the Maple Leafs' next game, which was in Toronto.

Toronto! Stanley looked around at the packed stadium. Hundreds of fans were waving signs. Suddenly he had a terrific idea. "Do you think you can hold me up if I stand on your shoulders?" he asked Nick.

Nick flexed his muscles. "Of course! I'm probably the strongest kid here!" He caught Mountie Martin's warning look, and then he said, "Well, you're pretty strong, too, Stanley." He made a step out of his hands. "Here, I'll give you a boost."

"Not yet," said Stanley. He pulled his red scarf way down over his face and pulled his red turtleneck up to meet it. And then to Nick and Mountie Martin's amazement, he folded his upper body into a perfect maple leaf. He pleated his legs, in their brown pants, into a stem!

"I learned origami while I was in Japan not long ago," came Stanley's muffled voice from somewhere inside the leaf. "Now hoist me up, Nick!"

Nick did, and the crowd went wild.

"There's our winner!" shouted the announcer. "No question at all! Come on down to the ice!"

Nick, holding the Stanley–maple leaf up in triumph, made his way down to the rink, surrounded by the admiring crowd. When he reached the centerline, Stanley jumped down and unfurled himself. And the fans went wild.

When the applause finally died down, the captain of the Maple Leafs skated over and handed Nick a puck and a hockey stick.

Stanley whispered something to Nick. Then Nick handed the puck back to the team captain. "No thanks," he said. "We'll use our own!"

And then Stanley lay down on the ice and coiled himself into a tight disk. Nick took aim and swung the hockey stick hard, whacking Stanley on the soles of his boots. Stanley skittered crazily across the ice. He was hurtling for the side line—nowhere near the goal. Stanley quickly calculated the angle and adjusted himself. When he hit the boards, he ricocheted off, now aiming right for the . . .

"Goal!" yelled the announcer. "I don't believe my eyes, but these two boys have just done the impossible!"

"You did the impossible, Stanley," Nick said when Stanley uncoiled himself. "Mountie Martin was right. . . . We really do make a good team!"

The captain of the team skated over and shook both boys' hands. He handed them the box seat tickets and airline tickets. "See you in Toronto!" he said.

Over the Falls!

The next morning, bright and early, Stanley and Nick bid good-bye to Mountie Martin at the airport and boarded the plane. "Whatever happens at Niagara Falls," they told each other, "we're already like brothers."

The flight was pleasant, but with nothing to distract them, both boys began to worry about their families

again. Where had they gone? How would they ever be reunited?

By the time they landed, Stanley and Nick were very homesick indeed.

An airport shuttle bus whisked them to Niagara Falls. As soon as they stepped off the bus, the boys heard the powerful waterfalls crashing in the distance. They couldn't see anything except a great cloud of misty spray, though. They headed for the sound, along with a crush of tourists.

As they walked, the boys passed several signs. "Look, Nick," Stanley pointed one out. "The falls are more than one hundred and seventy feet high here."

"One hundred and fifty thousand gallons of water goes over the crest line every second," Nick read on another.

Just then the mist cleared. The boys stared in wonder at the majestic sight of Niagara Falls, thundering beside them in a curtain of rainbows.

Nick ran to the railing. "Come here, Stanley!" he cried over the roar. "It's awesome!"

Stanley rushed to catch up. But when he reached the edge, he began to flap in the winds churned up by the rushing water. How could he have forgotten his problems with wind so soon? A sudden gust lifted him and plastered him to a signpost dangerously close to the edge.

Stanley tried to slither down, but the wind held him tight.

Nick climbed up onto the rail to try to peel him off. "You're the first friend I've ever had," he cried. "The only one who's put up with my bragging. I'm not about to lose you now!"

But as he struggled to push Stanley down to safety, Nick lost his footing on the mist-slicked metal. Over the railing he went, hurtling through the air, straight for the crashing waterfalls below!

Stanley didn't think for a second. He launched himself out, reached Nick in midair, and curved himself around his new friend. Like a barrel!

Together they crashed into the churning water. Over and over and over they smashed and battered against the rocks and angry waters.

Finally, the terrible tumbling stopped, and all was still blackness.

8

Together Again

Stanley awoke to find his parents' faces hovering above him. He rubbed his eyes. . . . Was this a dream? Or worse— was he . . . dead?

"My goodness, dear, you gave us quite a fright!" said his mother.

"Mom! Dad! What are you doing here?" Stanley asked.

"Don't you remember?" Mr.

Lambchop asked. "When you were up so high at the snowboarding championships, you kept yelling, 'We're going to the Falls!' 'We're going to the Falls!' We would never have allowed it if we'd known you were planning to go *in*to the falls, though! We just thought you'd meet us here for the wedding."

"What? No, that, was Nick. He was yelling . . . oh, never mind. The important thing is that you're here! I'm so glad to see you! But, hey, where *is* Nick?"

"Hay is for horses, dear," Mrs. Lambchop reminded him. "Do try to remember that. Nick is over there. His father is examining him now."

Doctor Dave came over then. "My boy's fine," he said. "How about I take a look at yours, Lambchops?"

"Please do!" said Mr. and Mrs. Lambchop at the same time.

Doctor Dave gave Stanley a thorough examination. Then he called Stanley's parents back over. "No broken bones, that's the good news," he began.

"Oh, dear!" Mrs. Lambchop exclaimed. "If there's bad news, you'd better give it to us right away. Delaying it won't make it any easier." Harriet Lambchop was both very practical and very brave.

"Well, here it is, then," Doctor Dave said. "The repeated violent impact with the rushing water has flattened your son. Water trauma can do that. That's why you don't see anyone swimming around here. I can't tell how long the flatness will last, but you should be prepared for the worst."

"But, Doctor Dave, Stanley was flat *before* all this," Mrs. Lambchop said. "So if that's all, then he's fine!"

Doctor Dave patted Mrs. Lambchop's hand. "Denial. Very common in cases like this. You just keep thinking whatever you need to think in order to get through it. Well, I must be off. . . . Nick and I have a wedding to get to."

"Why, so do we!" Mrs. Lambchop said. "I know a lot of people get married at Niagara Falls, but do you suppose it's the same wedding?"

Wonder of wonders, it was! The bride was an old college chum of Nick's mother, Shelby Smith. The groom was an old college chum of Stanley's father, Ralph Jones. Their families sat on different sides of the aisle, but Stanley watched with pride as his new friend, Nick, carried the ring for the bride and groom.

Afterward, at the reception, Stanley, Nick, and Arthur

had a wonderful time together. Doctor Dave had been right about Arthur's ankle—a few days of rest and it was as good as new.

After a while, Mr. and Mrs. Lambchop came over to fetch the boys. "It's time we congratulated the newlyweds."

As they walked over, Stanley told Nick about the groom. "Mr. Jones has a remarkable memory. . . . He never forgets anything!"

And sure enough, when they reached Mr. Jones, he astonished them with his perfect recall. "Hello there, Stanley," he said. "What do you hear from Egypt? That Sir Abu Shenti Hawara the fourth still in prison for trying to rob the tomb of Pharaoh Khufufull?"

Mr. Lambchop came up then. "Congratulations, Ralph," he said, shaking his friend's hand. "That wonderful memory of yours should make for a happy marriage, I predict. At least you'll never forget your anniversary!"

"Let's hope so," Ralph Jones said. "But, you know, my excellent memory is the very thing that kept me from marrying Shelby years ago." Here he paused to gaze down at his bride fondly. "All that time apart . . . what a waste!" He sighed.

"What happened?" Stanley asked.

"We went to high school together.

I remembered that once, at a football game, Shelby had smiled fetchingly at the star quarterback. His name was B. F. Wellington. Big fellow. Everyone called him Beef. Beef Wellington . . . get it? Har, har. Except my heart was broken. . . . Shelby had smiled at him, not me. For all those years, Shelby denied it. But then finally, she admitted she *had* smiled at him . . . but only to make me jealous. So I forgave her and asked her to be my bride."

The new Mr. and Mrs. Jones kissed each other then.

"In a marriage," Mrs. Lambchop advised the groom, "forgiveness is much more important than memory."

"That sounds like good advice," Mr. Jones said. "I'll try to remember that."

That evening, the Lambchops enjoyed the Maple Leafs' game very much. But all four of them agreed they were even happier to return home that evening.

Stanley thumbtacked a newspaper clipping to the bulletin board over his bed. "OVER THE FALLS IS NO BARREL OF LAUGHS FOR TWO BRAVE BOYS," read the headline.

"That was quite a vacation," Stanley said. "I wish you

could have made the trip with me, though, Arthur."

"It was my fault," Arthur said. "I was showing off on the ski slope. And Stanley . . . I'm sorry for all the teasing about your shape."

"That's all right," Stanley replied. "Actually, it's kind of *flat*-tering."

He turned off the lamp, and the two brothers lay in their beds chuckling for a few minutes about Stanley's joke. And then they fell fast asleep.

THE END

WHAT YOU NEED TO KNOW TO BE A ROYAL CANADIAN MOUNTIE

The name *Canada* likely originated from *kanata*, the Huron-Iroquois word for "village" or "settlement."

There are two official languages in Canada: English and French. But about six million Canadians don't speak either language!

Canada has 8,893 kilometers (5,525 miles) of border and shares all of it with only one country, and that's the US!

Acting as a border in the east for Canada and the US is Niagara Falls. It is the most powerful series of waterfalls in North America, and many daredevils have tried to survive a drop over the edge. In 1901, Annie Edson Taylor was the first person to go over the perilous Falls—in a barrel.

Bordered by three oceans—the Atlantic, Pacific, and Arctic—the world's longest coastline belongs to Canada. It's 243,042 kilometers (15,102 miles) long.

Canada's official winter sport is ice hockey, and the tradition of the Stanley Cup trophy began in Canada. The Montreal Canadiens have won 24 Stanley Cup titles—more than any other team.

The Stanley Cup spends approximately 250 days a year traveling. It has ventured off to many countries, including the Czech Republic, Sweden, Russia, Finland, Japan, Switzerland, and the Bahamas. It even has bodyguards!

Spanning 44,807 square kilometers (over 11 million acres), the Wood Buffalo National Park is Canada's biggest national park and one of the world's most vast. It protects the largest bison herd and is home to the only nesting site of the whooping crane.

Read the Stories That Started It All!

A Flat Boy Can Do Almost Anything!

Stanley Lambchop is an ordinary boy. At least he was, until the night his bulletin board fell off the wall and flattened him. All of a sudden, Stanley can slide under doors, mail himself across the country in an envelope, and fly like a kite!

But flatness has its serious side, too. Sneak thieves have been stealing paintings from the Famous Museum of Art, and Stanley knows he's the only one who can stop them. Will the robbers discover Stanley's plan before he foils theirs?

Have You Seen Stanley?

One morning, after a dark and stormy night, Stanley Lambchop is nowhere to be found. But wait . . . what is that boy-shaped lump underneath his bedsheets? And where's that giggling coming from? It's Stanley and he's . . . invisible!

At first there are great adventures for an invisible boy to have. Stanley becomes an unseen helper in a bike race, on a television show, and even fighting crime! But then Stanley starts to miss being seen, and wonders if he will stay invisible forever. . . .

Stanley Lambchop Is Out of This World!

The United States has received a message from distant planet Tyrra: *Will you meet with us?* The President wants to send someone who is friendly, but also someone brave, adventurous, and clever—who better than Stanley Lambchop?

The whole Lambchop family bundles into the *Star Scout* spaceship with Stanley as Chief Pilot to voyage to far-off Tyrra. But do the Tyrrans simply want a friendly meeting? Or did they lure these intergalactic visitors for another, secret reason?

Stanley's Back and Flatter Than Ever!

Stanley Lambchop thought he was back to being a normal, round boy for good—until one morning when, out of nowhere, he seems to have gone flat. *Again.* While being half an inch thick has its interesting points, Stanley can't help wondering why he can't just be like everybody else.

But when disaster strikes downtown and one of Stanley's classmates is trapped, Stanley discovers that being different can definitely come in handy. After all, sometimes it takes a flat hero to save the day.

And Check Out Flat Stanley's Worldwide Adventures!

Saddle Up with Flat Stanley

Ever since Stanley was flattened by a bulletin board, every trip is an adventure!

The whole Lambchop family is off to see Mount Rushmore. But when Flat Stanley and his brother, Arthur, team up with a scrappy cowgirl named Calamity Jasper, their vacation turns into the Wild West experience of a lifetime. Pretty soon, they find themselves in a real tight spot—even for a flat boy like Stanley!

Ancient Pyramids Can Be Flat-out Dangerous!

Because Stanley's been flattened by a bulletin board, there are places he can get to that no one else can. So when Stanley receives a letter from an archaeologist, he travels by airmail to Egypt to help find an ancient treasure deep in the heart of a great pyramid. But what if even the flattest boy on earth can't wriggle out of this dark tomb—and the terrible mess he finds himself in?

A Flat Ninja?

Stanley and his brother, Arthur, are such huge fans of the movie star ninja Oda Nobu that they decide to send him something even better than fan mail— Stanley himself! Soon enough, Flat Stanley is in Japan, seeing the country with his idol. But when trouble surprises them, it will take a real hero to save the day.

THERE'S NO PLACE ON EARTH THAT A FLAT KID CAN'T GO!
Don't miss:

TURN THE PAGE FOR A SNEAK PEEK!

¡OLÉ!

"You have met your match!" Stanley Lambchop called down the hallway to his younger brother, Arthur.

Arthur snorted and stomped his foot.

"My *amigo* is right!" said Carlos, their friend from next door. Stanley knew that "*amigo*" meant "friend" in Spanish. "You will never defeat great matadors like us!"

Carlos took Stanley's hands and dangled him just off the ground. This was not very difficult, because Carlos was quite tall for his age. Also, Stanley was only half an inch thick.

Stanley had been flat ever since the enormous bulletin board over his bed fell on him one night while he was sleeping. Sometimes he found being flat no fun at all. People had a habit of sitting on him on the bus. But there were good things about being flat, too. Stanley could slide under doors. He could travel inexpensively through the mail. And he could be a very good bullfighter's cape whenever Carlos came over to play.

Arthur charged down the hall, headed straight for them. At the very last moment, Carlos swung Stanley upward. Arthur passed below as Stanley's toes brushed the ceiling.

"¡Olé!" Carlos and Stanley cried

triumphantly. They turned to face their opponent.

Arthur narrowed his eyes and slowly backed up to the other end of the hall.

Stanley knew to take his brother very seriously when Arthur was mad. After all, it wasn't always easy for Arthur, having a brother who was flat and could do so many unusual things. Plus, Stanley was dressed all in red, which Carlos said made bulls angry.

With a roar, Arthur rushed toward them. He was the fastest bull Stanley had ever seen in their house. Carlos tightened his grip on Stanley's hands.

Stanley took a deep breath and—

"BOYS!!" a voice bellowed right

behind them as Carlos swept Stanley through the air.

It was Mr. Lambchop! Stanley was about to swing right into him!

Stanley pointed his toes as hard as he could. They skidded against the ceiling, bringing him to a stop.

The good news was that Stanley Lambchop had not crashed into his father. The bad news was that he was now upside down and face-to-face with him.

"Haven't I told you, 'No horsing around?!'" Mr. Lambchop said.

"But we weren't playing horses, Dad!" protested Arthur.

Mrs. Lambchop appeared from the

kitchen. "Arthur is right, dear," she said. "One shouldn't call it horseplay when they were playing bullfight." Practicing proper speech was one of Mr. and Mrs. Lambchop's favorite activities.

"My cousin Carmen del Junco is a famous matador in Mexico," Carlos admitted. "It is in my blood."

"Speaking of Mexico," Mrs. Lambchop said, smiling, "guess what's for breakfast."

Everyone followed her into the kitchen. "What is it?" Stanley asked, poking the yellow mound on his plate with a fork. It certainly smelled good.

"Why, it's *huevos rancheros*!" Mrs. Lambchop said.

"Looks more like eggs," said Arthur.

Carlos chuckled. "*'Huevos'* means 'eggs' in Spanish. *Huevos rancheros* is a special dish with eggs on top of a tortilla." He elbowed Stanley. "You will like the tortilla, *amigo*. It is flat like you!"

BECAUSE GEOGRAPHY CAN BE FLAT-OUT AMAZING!

Travel to www.flatstanleybooks.com for games, global facts, pen pal opportunities, and more activities for kids, parents, and classrooms!